ADAPTED BY TRACEY WEST

SCHOLASTIC INC.
New York Toronto London Auckland Sydney
Mexico City New Delhi Hong Kong Buenos Aires

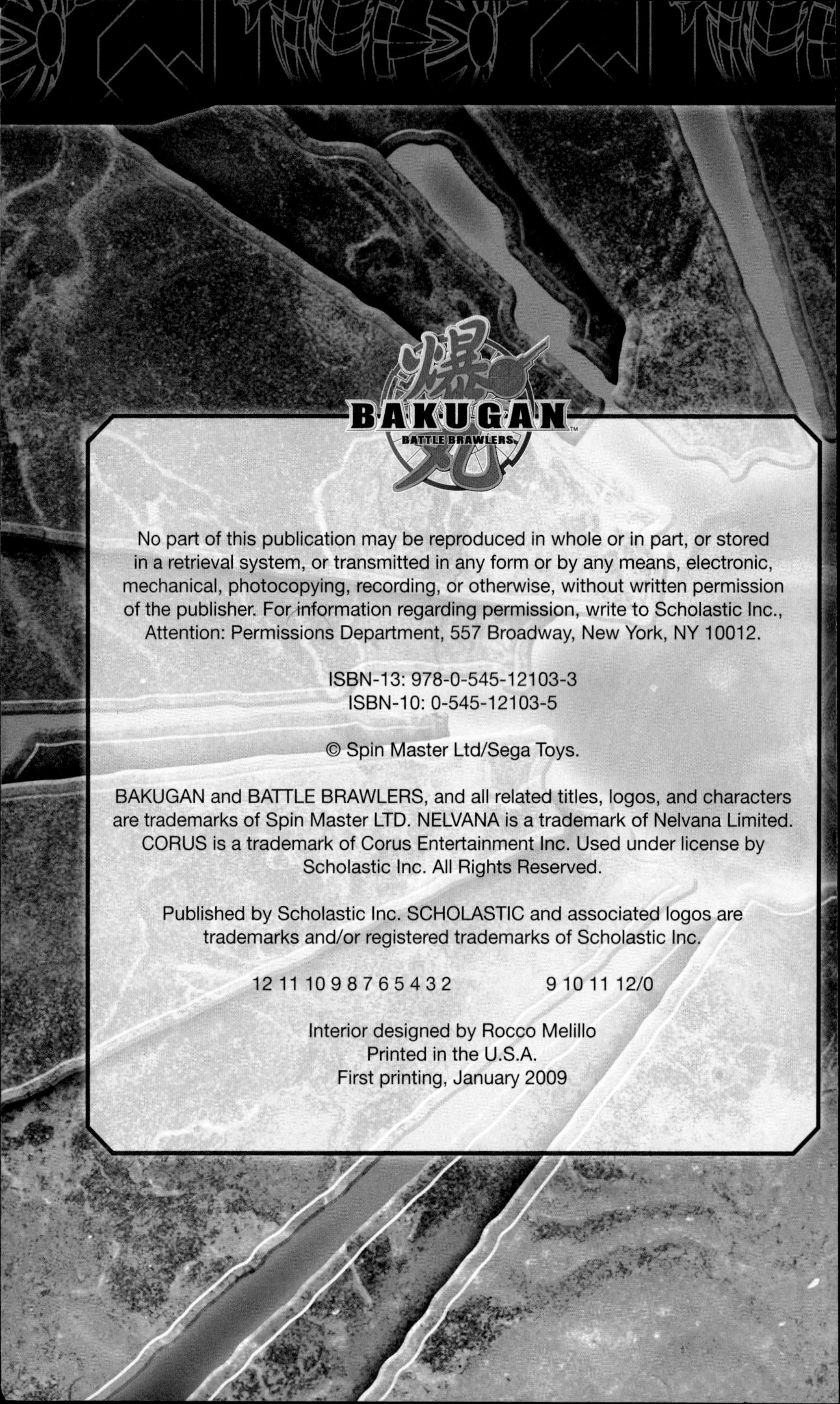

ISBN-13: 978-0-545-12103-3
ISBN-10: 0-545-12103-5

Published by Scholastic Inc. SCHOLASTIC and associated logos are trademarks and/or registered trademarks of Scholastic Inc.

12 11 10 9 8 7 6 5 4 3 2 9 10 11 12/0

Interior designed by Rocco Melillo
Printed in the U.S.A.
First printing, January 2009

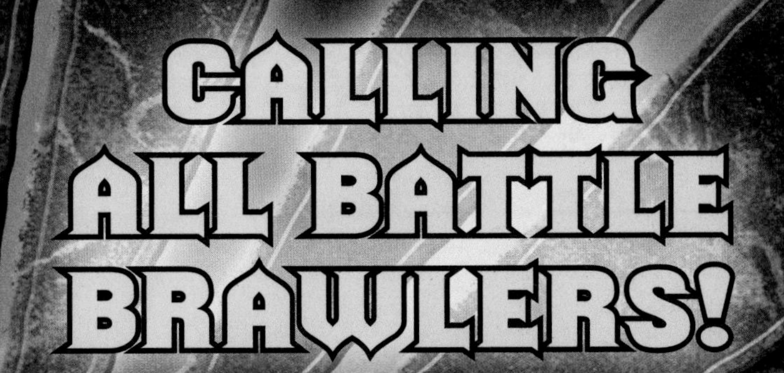

CALLING ALL BATTLE BRAWLERS!

Do you think about Bakugan when you wake up in the morning and dream about it at night? Do you scout your schoolyard to see if it will make a good Bakugan field? When you're eating dinner, do you have the urge to shoot your meatballs across the table and yell, "Bakugan Brawl!"?

Don't worry. You're not alone! The Bakugan craze is sweeping the planet. Brawlers everywhere are challenging each other to brawl with their Bakugan warriors and Bakugan cards.

The next time you head to a brawl, make sure you have this guide book in your pocket. It's got everything you want to know about Bakugan inside. You'll learn about the Bakugan warriors and how they get their powers. You'll meet some top brawlers and find out what makes them tick. You'll also pick up some tips and strategies for playing the game.

So have fun checking out this book and then . . . let the brawling begin!

HEY! MY NAME IS DAN

I know this is gonna sound weird, but one day my whole world changed. These cards started dropping from the sky like rain. At first we didn't know where they were coming from or who sent them. We only knew they were more than just ordinary playing cards. And it was happening all over the world!

Together with my online friends from around the world, we invented a wicked new game called Bakugan. That's when the power of the cards was revealed. Each one held its own battling beast that came to life when you threw it down. The battles were intense and if you chose the wrong card, you lost it *and* your Bakugan warrior.

But that's only half the story. Another even bigger battle was taking place in a parallel universe called Vestroia. Vestroia is the home world of the Bakugan warriors. The universe gets its power from two sources: the Infinity Core and the Silent Core. A power-hungry Dragonoid beast named Naga wanted all of that power for himself. He tried to steal it, but failed. He swallowed the Silent Core, a source of negative energy. The Infinity Core, a source of positive energy, fell to Earth.

And that's not all that fell. Many Bakugan fell through the gate between the worlds that day. These warriors were different than the beasts on the cards—they could talk to their owners. That's how I got my Bakugan, Drago.

Naga wanted to find the Infinity Core badly. He sent a human named Masquerade to find it for him. He also wanted Masquerade to send Bakugan to the Doom Dimension so he could steal their energy.

That's when I learned that brawling was much more than a game. Together with my friends Runo, Marucho, Shun, Julie, and Alice, we decided to stop Masquerade—and save the world. We've also got to save our Bakugan from the Doom Dimension. Hey, it's a big job, but somebody's got to do it, right?

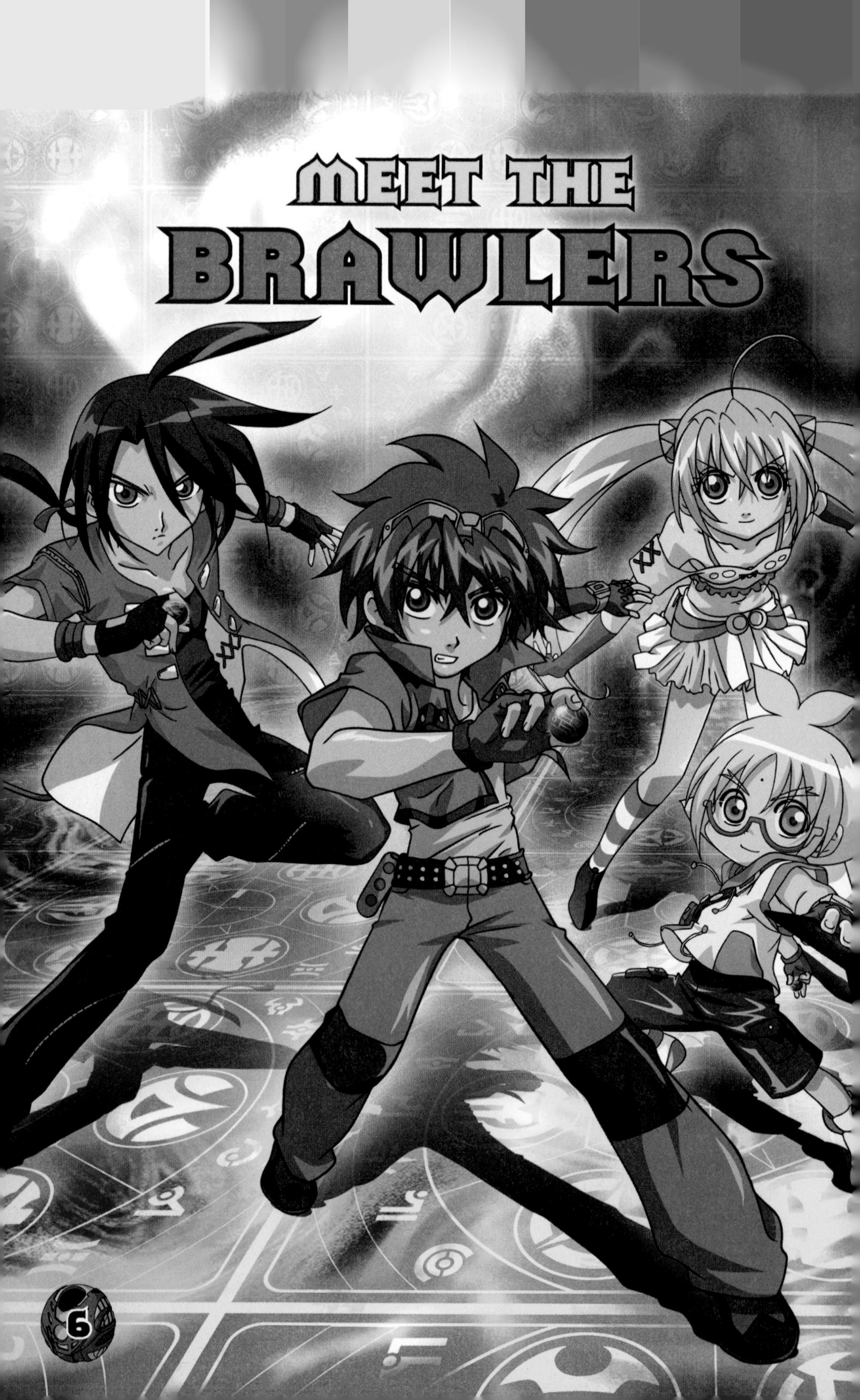
MEET THE
BRAWLERS

When Bakugan cards fell from the sky, they landed in countries all over the world. Kids everywhere became Bakugan brawlers.

Brawlers are as different as the Bakugan they battle with. Some are boys and some are girls. Some are brainy and some are bullies. Some are nice and some are sinister.

But the very best brawlers all have one thing in common: They combine skill and strategy when they battle with their Bakugan. Good brawlers need to be able to make fast decisions—especially when it's time to throw a Bakugan on the field. They have to know which cards to use when their Bakugan needs more power.

Skill and strategy are not all a brawler needs. The third ingredient? Confidence. It's easy to get discouraged when you lose your first Bakugan in a brawl. The best brawlers know not to give up until the last Bakugan stands.

In this section you'll meet Dan and his friends and their Guardian Bakugan. You'll also meet a few of Dan's opponents—including Masquerade, who wants to send all Bakugan to the Doom Dimension!

Read on to check out what makes these brawlers tick. Maybe you can learn a few tricks!

DAN
AGE: 12
BRAWLING STYLE:
A master of power play, Dan likes to use the biggest, baddest Bakugan to take down his opponents.

Along with Shun, Dan invented the rules of the Bakugan game. Dan lives for Bakugan. He talks about it at school, he plays it during his free time, and he dreams about it at night.

Dan likes to use fire attributes in battle, and they're a perfect match for his fiery personality. Dan has a lot of energy and always wants to battle. But he's hot-headed, and when things don't go his way, he can easily lose his cool. That can sometimes cause Dan to lose a brawl.

Dan's short temper might be the reason he has never been number one in the Bakugan rankings. It's the thing he wants most, and he won't stop until he gets to the top.

DAN'S GUARDIAN BAKUGAN: Drago

BEST KNOWN FOR: Drago can give off intense heat that dissolves everything around him.

ULTIMATE ABILITY CARD:
Boosted Dragon powers Drago with 50 extra Gs. Drago is a Dragonoid Bakugan attributed to the world of fire, Pyrus. In the dimension known as Vestroia, he acted as leader of the Bakugan. Level-headed Drago believed Vestroia should be kept separate from the human world. That all changed, of course, when Naga ripped open a portal, and Drago got sucked into the human world. Now Drago battles for Dan. The two don't always get along, but Drago is loyal to Dan and has helped Dan win many brawls. Drago is extremely powerful and has the ability to evolve on his own.

Shun doesn't talk a lot—but on the field, he doesn't have to. He brawls with the effortless skill of a seasoned pro. Maybe that's because he helped invent the rules of the game. Or maybe he takes after his grandfather, a famous ninja warrior.

For a long time, Shun was the number one ranked Bakugan brawler. Then the mysterious Masquerade showed up and stole the title from him. Shun had to go through a lot to get back on top again.

SHUN'S GUARDIAN BAKUGAN: Ventus Skyress

BEST KNOWN FOR: Like a phoenix, Skyress has the amazing power to resurrect when defeated.

ULTIMATE ABILITY CARD: Green Nobility Violent Wind increases this Bakugan's power by 100 Gs.

Only a master brawler like Shun could handle a Bakugan like Ventus Skyress. Gaining power from the wind, Skyress brawls with her huge wings and long tails, which end in sharp feathers. Besides the ability to resurrect, Skyress can also see into the future—and see through objects, too.

SHUN

AGE: 13

BRAWLING STYLE:
Like a ninja, Shun carefully calculates every move.

MARUCHO

AGE: 11

BATTLE STYLE:
Marucho believes that if you memorize the data for each Bakugan, you can't lose.

Marucho has everything a kid could ever want—a huge mansion, the most expensive computers, even a personal zoo. But nothing means more to him than Bakugan, and the brawlers who are his friends.

Marucho might be small, but he's got a big brain. It's crammed with data about every Bakugan and Bakugan card on Earth. He uses that knowledge to strategize in battle. Sometimes, though, it takes more than facts to win a brawl—you need to learn to trust your instincts, too. Marucho needs to trust himself—and he might learn that lesson the hard way.

MARUCHO'S GUARDIAN BAKUGAN: Aquos Preyas

BEST KNOWN FOR: Preyas has an unusual ability to change attributes.

ULTIMATE ABILITY CARD: Blue Stealth. This card takes 50 Gs from your opponent's Bakugan, and adds 50 Gs to yours.

Preyas might look like some kind of monster you'd find in a slimy swamp, but he'd rather make you laugh than scare you. He can change how he gains his power, whether it's from fire, earth, light, darkness, water, or wind. Preyas likes to see the look of surprise on his opponents' faces when he makes the switch.

Preyas likes to goof around, but he's serious about his loyalty to Marucho. Preyas and Marucho both admire each other. It makes them good friends—and a great combination on the field.

When Julie brawls, her opponents sometimes think she's going to be easy to beat. Maybe it's because she's so pretty, or because she can be a little flighty. She's always smiling, even when she's feeling sad.

But when it's time to brawl . . . watch out! Julie slams the opposition with powerful Subterra Bakugan. The Bakugan across the field don't know what hit them, and Julie walks away a winner—with a smile on her face, of course.

JULIE'S GUARDIAN BAKUGAN:
Subterra Gorem

BEST KNOWN FOR:
A super-tough exterior makes him hard to take down.

ULTIMATE ABILITY CARD:
Mega Impact boosts Gorem with an extra 50 Gs.

Subterra Gorem looks like a big brute carved out of rock. He gets his power from the Subterra world—which means he's infused with the energy of the Earth. His body is made of extremely hard cells that are difficult to penetrate.

Gorem might look big and bad, but inside he's a real softie. He's gentle and will do whatever Julie asks. He does have a mean temper though, and when it comes out, only Julie can calm him down.

JULIE

AGE: 12

BATTLE STYLE: A master of direct attacks, Julie relies on the power of her Bakugan rather than strategy.

RUNO
AGE: 12
BATTLE STYLE:
Runo combines power moves with smart strategy.

Runo is an only child. Her parents own a restaurant, and when Runo's not brawling, she works as a waitress there. She likes to battle with Bakugan who have light attributes from the planet Haos.

Dan and Runo are alike in some ways. They both love Bakugan, and Runo is energetic and impatient, too. She gets angry when she loses. When she plays on a team, she'll sometimes make a move without checking with her team members. Runo and Dan make a good team on the field.

RUNO'S GUARDIAN BAKUGAN: Haos Tigrerra

BEST KNOWN FOR: The blade inside Tigrerra's body can cut through anything in the human world.

ULTIMATE ABILITY CARD: Crystal Fang gives Tigrerra an 80 G power boost.

Runo's Haos Tigrerra is smart and polite off the field. On the field, Tigrerra goes wild! She's a powerful beast who gives everything she's got in battle. Her opponents know they've got to bring out their best game when they see Tigrerra's sharp claws and strong muscles.

Tigrerra is devoted to Runo and trusts her completely. She will protect Runo no matter what it takes.

You won't often find Alice brawling with her Bakugan, but when Dan and his friends need advice, she's always online to help out. Even though she lives in Russia, getting brawling tips from Alice is just a few clicks of a mouse away.

Alice has a special ability most brawlers would love to have, too. She can see the Gs of any Bakugan on the field! That gives her an extra edge in battle.

Thanks to a dose of dark energy, Alice's body was the host for the mysterious brawler, Masquerade. Poor Alice didn't even know she had another identity. When Masquerade was finally defeated, Alice was left with his Darkus Hydranoid, which evolved into an Ultimate Hydranoid after gobbling up energy from the Doom Dimension.

ALICE

AGE: 14

BATTLE STYLE:
Like Marucho, Alice likes to study Bakugan so she can use strategy in battle.

MASQUERADE

AGE: Unknown

BATTLE STYLE:
Masquerade relies on Doom Cards to cause the ultimate destruction of his opponents.

When this masked brawler came on the scene, nobody was sure what he was after. Then Masquerade began using his Doom Cards to send opposing Bakugan to the Doom Dimension forever. Dan and his friends quickly figured out that Masquerade was collecting energy for Naga. Like the evil scientist Hal-G, Masquerade wants to help Naga become the ruler of Vestroia and Earth.

Masquerade has no mercy for his opponents. He prefers Bakugan with Darkus attributes—and he knows how to use them. How many Bakugan will Masquerade send to the Doom Dimension before he is stopped?

MASQUERADE'S GUARDIAN BAKUGAN: Darkus Hydranoid

BEST KNOWN FOR: Darkus Hydranoid is bad to the bone.

This hulking beast might be slow-moving, but Darkus Hydranoid has a mean streak that makes him ruthless on the field. The sharp spines on his body can do a lot of damage to an opponent.

Why is Hydranoid so vicious on the field? You can thank his master for that. Masquerade has complete control over Hydranoid. This Darkus Bakugan can't make a move on his own, so he's got to do whatever Masquerade tells him to do.

Alice's grandfather Michael isn't a brawler. He's a scientist who studies Bakugan. Michael was curious when Bakugan began to fall from the sky, so he launched an investigation.

Michael made an important discovery. He learned that Bakugan come from another dimension called Vestroia. Then he found the portal that links Vestroia to Earth.

What was the Vestroia dimension like? Michael wanted to know, so he transported himself there. Disaster struck when he got sucked into the evil energy of the Silent Core, one of Vestroia's power sources. This energy transformed Michael into Hal-G—and that's when things started to get nasty!

RESEARCHER

MICHAEL

HAL-C

Some people say that when Alice's grandfather Michael got zapped with evil energy, he became a creature that was half-human, half-Bakugan. Hal-G certainly doesn't look like a normal human, so this may be true.

Hal-G is the loyal servant of Naga, a Dragonoid who wants ultimate power over both Vestroia and Earth. To do that, Naga needs the Infinity Core, and Hal-G will do anything to help him get it.

HAL-G'S GUARDIAN BAKUGAN: Naga

BEST KNOWN FOR: It is rumored that Naga's power reaches an incredible 1000 Gs.

Naga's dreams of ultimate power took shape when he got his claws on the human scientist Michael. After Michael transformed into the evil Hal-G, Naga used Hal-G to help him reach his goals.

Naga wants to rule both Earth and Vestroia. He's willing to destroy every Bakugan to get what he wants. Drago tried to reason with Naga, but Naga wouldn't listen. After Naga absorbed the Silent Core, he became so evil there was no sense in talking to him. The only way to stop Naga would be on the Bakugan battle-field. But how do you fight a beast that's packed with power?

Joe is the webmaster of the Bakugan website. He's a whiz on the computer, but not so big on brawling. He'd rather find out what other brawlers are up to.

Because Joe knows so much about the Bakugan brawlers, Dan and his friends thought he might be a spy for Masquerade. But Joe proved them wrong, and then joined the quest to stop Masquerade for good. Because he knows so much, he's a useful member of the team.

BILLY

Billy and Julie have known each other since they were kids. They both like Bakugan with Subterra attributes. But when Billy came under Masquerade's control, Julie found herself facing her old friend on the field.

Billy is a master brawler and has ranked as high as tenth in the world. He has teamed up with brawler Komba. On the field, he uses his powerful Subterra Cycloid to take down opponents.

KOMBA

Komba lives in Nairobi, Africa, but he'll travel the world for a good Bakugan battle. He battled Shun twice, and lost both times. Then he asked Shun to be his teacher.

Like Billy, Komba fell under Masquerade's control. He's smart on the field, and has been ranked as high as fifth place. His guardian Bakugan is a Ventus Harpus, a winged beast with sharp fangs.

Klaus is one of the best brawlers in the world—only Shun and Masquerade have ranked higher than him. His family is so rich he lives in a castle. This combination of wealth and skill makes Klaus kind of a show-off.

Klaus became Masquerade's top henchman. With the help of his Bakugan, Aquos Sirenoid, he battled Dan and his friends. In one battle, he took control of Marucho's guardian Bakugan, Preyas.

CHAN

Chan is an expert brawler who has been ranked third in the world. That made her a target for Masquerade, who held her under his control. With Klaus and Julio, she battled Dan, Marucho, and Runo. Chan's guardian Bakugan is a Pyrus Fourtress.

JULIO

Masquerade's muscleman Julio is a big guy who makes big moves on the field. He battles with his Haos Tentaclear, a beast with one eye and six tentacles. Julio reached number four in the Bakugan rankings.

VESTROIA AND ITS PLANETS

Imagine a place where all Bakugan roam in their warrior form. They bathe in raging rivers. They bask in blazing fires. They soar on savage winds. They live free, growing strong in body and spirit.

There is such a place, and it's called Vestroia. This universe is made up of six different planets. Each planet has a different attribute: fire, earth, water, air, light, and darkness. Each Bakugan comes from one of these planets and gets its power from that planet.

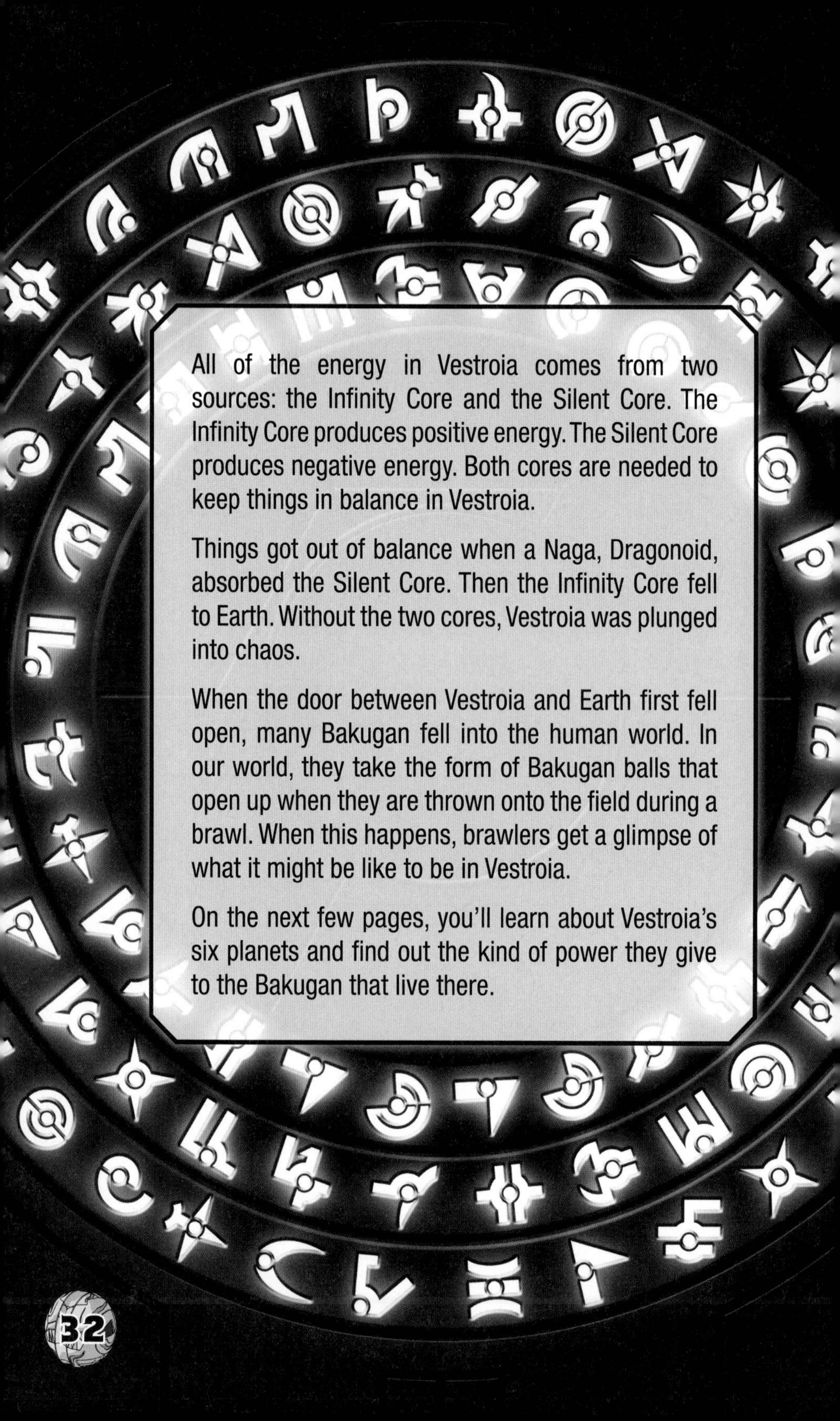

All of the energy in Vestroia comes from two sources: the Infinity Core and the Silent Core. The Infinity Core produces positive energy. The Silent Core produces negative energy. Both cores are needed to keep things in balance in Vestroia.

Things got out of balance when a Naga, Dragonoid, absorbed the Silent Core. Then the Infinity Core fell to Earth. Without the two cores, Vestroia was plunged into chaos.

When the door between Vestroia and Earth first fell open, many Bakugan fell into the human world. In our world, they take the form of Bakugan balls that open up when they are thrown onto the field during a brawl. When this happens, brawlers get a glimpse of what it might be like to be in Vestroia.

On the next few pages, you'll learn about Vestroia's six planets and find out the kind of power they give to the Bakugan that live there.

PYRUS

You have to travel deep into the center of Vestroia to find Pyrus. This planet constantly blazes with raging heat. Most Bakugan would burn up under these conditions, but Pyrus Bakugan thrive on it. They get their power from the heat and flames.

On the field, Pyrus Bakugan use this fire power to blast opponents with fiery attacks. Pyrus attacks are fast, hot, and furious.

Dan's opponents feel the heat when he battles with Pyrus Bakugan.

VENTUS

Ventus Bakugan get their power from the wind and the air. In Vestroia, they soar on the winds that blow on the surface of Ventus.

Ventus Bakugan can attack with the power of a whirling tornado. Like a storm, they can strike quickly, without warning.

Shun soars with his Ventus Bakugan.

AQUOS

The planet Aquos is covered in water. From space, the water looks calm and peaceful. But deep below the surface, Bakugan warriors battle and train.

Pyrus Bakugan can battle in any watery place—the sea, a lake, a river, you name it. Like water, they can flow from one attack position to the next on the field. And like a stormy ocean, they can unleash a tidal wave of power on their opponents.

Aquos Bakugan floats Marucho's boat.

SUBTERRA

On top of the planet Subterra you'll find rough, rocky plains, hills, and mountains. Below the surface are dark underground tunnels. Subterra Bakugan train above and below ground. This rugged planet really toughens them up.

Subterra Bakugan have rock-hard bodies. When they attack, they can smash opponents with the power of boulders. Their powerful attacks feel like earthquakes on the field.

Julie rocks every brawl with her Subterra Bakugan.

HAOS

You'd better put on shades if you go to the planet Haos. The bright light from this shining planet can hurt your eyes. The energy produced by this light is special. The planet is surrounded by a mystic aura that helps give Haos Bakugan their power.

On the field, Haos Bakugan can control light and energy. They can blind their opponents with explosive power.

Runo lights up the field with her Haos Bakugan.

DARKUS

Deep in the Dark Hemisphere of Vestroia is where you'll find the planet Darkus. It is always night on Darkus. The Bakugan who live here get their power from the gloom and shadows.

The darker it is, the stronger a Darkus Bakugan becomes. Some say the hearts of Darkus Bakugan are dark as well. They can be cruel on the field, causing ruthless destruction. Many seasoned brawlers get nervous when they see a Darkus Bakugan across the field.

Shadowy Masquerade likes to battle with Darkus Bakugan.

BAKUGAN WARRIORS

Every Bakugan gets its power from one of the six planets in Vestroia. Each Bakugan also belongs to a warrior class. There are almost fifty known classes of warriors in Vestroia—and more may be discovered as more Bakugan travel through the gate that leads to the human world.

Some warrior classes have the ability to evolve into new Bakugan. Some warriors can evolve on their own. Others need a special card to evolve. When a Bakugan evolves, it becomes a bigger, badder version of its former self.

KNOW YOUR NAMES

A Bakugan's name is usually a combination of the planet it comes from and its warrior class. So a Saurus from the planet Subterra is a Subterra Saurus. A Saurus from the planet Pyrus would be a Pyrus Saurus.

Some brawlers, like Dan, like to give their Bakugan nicknames. Dan calls his Pyrus Dragonoid "Drago" for short. What do you like to call your Bakugan?

APOLLONIR

Like Dan's Drago, Apollonir is a Pyrus Dragonoid. This legendary warrior is the leader of the famed six warriors of Vestroia.

BEE STRIKER

This warrior looks like a bee—a really big bee! And a really big bee has a really big sting, of course.

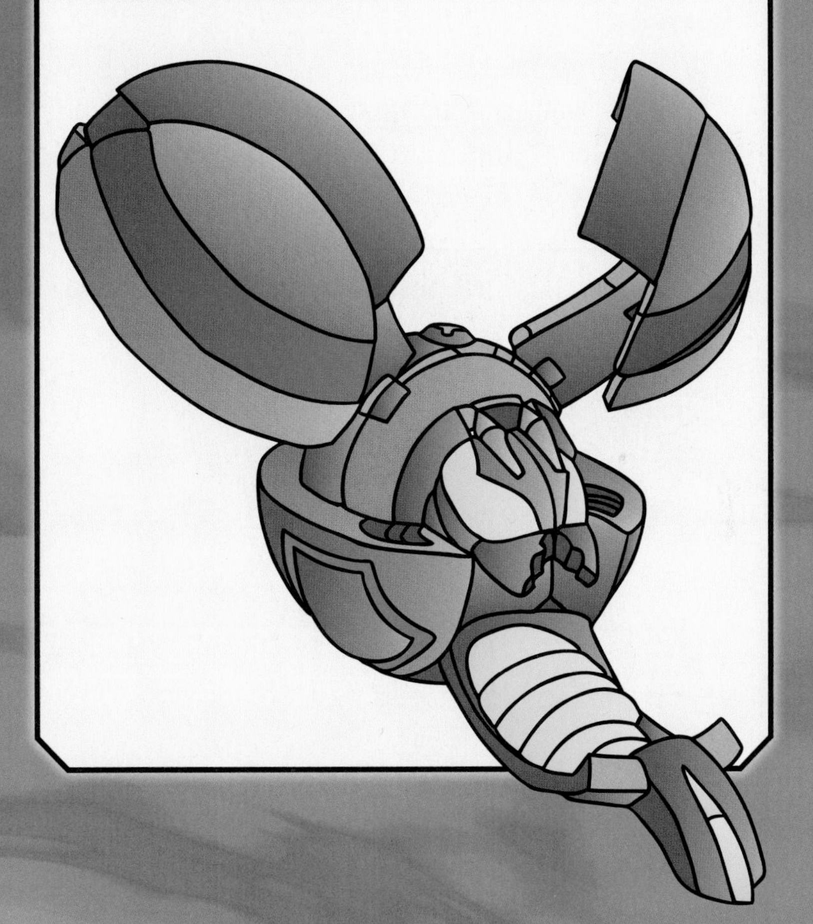

BLADE TIGRERRA

Forget about claws! Blade Tigrerra is ready for battle with a body studded with super-sharp blades. The evolved form of Tigrerra, this tigerlike terror walks on two legs.

CENTIPOID

You may want to bug out when you encounter this scary Bakugan. If the sight of all those legs isn't enough to spook you, this creature's giant pincers will have you running for cover.

CLAYF

One of the six legendary soldiers of Vestroia, Clayf is a Subterra Bakugan. Clayf is said to be the strongest of the six soldiers. This warrior has a rock-hard body made of clay.

CYCLOID

This is one eye-normous Bakugan! The colossal Cycloid carries a huge hammer in his right hand. When Cycloid swings its hammer, brace yourself. This powerful Bakugan packs quite a wallop.

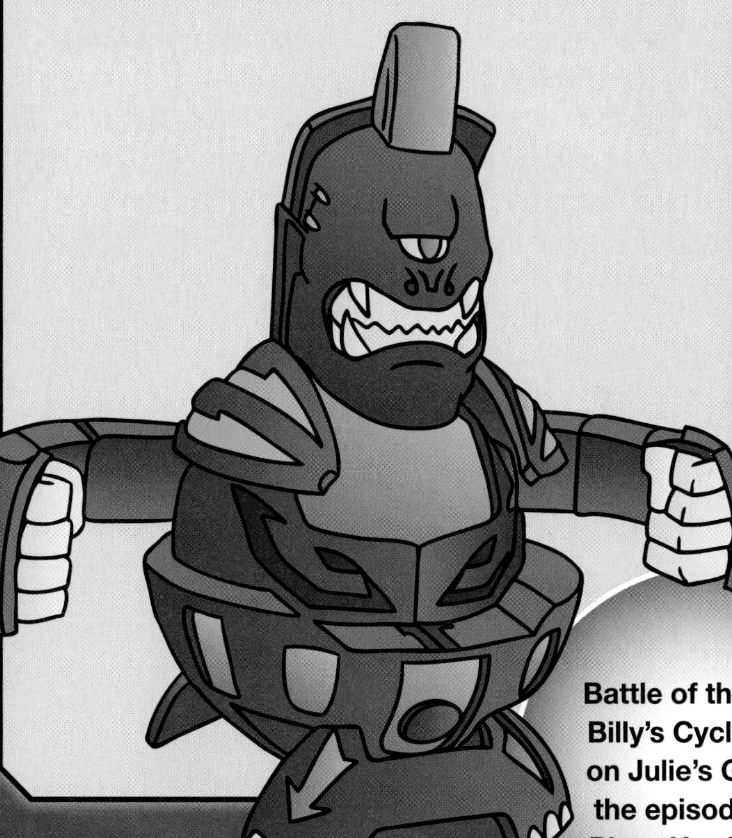

Battle of the giants! Billy's Cycloid took on Julie's Gorem in the episode "Julie Plays Hard Brawl."

DRAGONOID

With wicked clawed hands and feet and a super-sharp horn, a Dragonoid is a Bakugan to be reckoned with. Don't even bother to try hiding from this creature. A Dragonoid is an expert at seek-and-destroy combat. Highly intelligent, Dragonoids may not be the most agile Bakugan, but they make up for it with their powerful attacks.

DELTA DRAGONOID

Dragonoid is one of a few Bakugan than can evolve on its own. Delta Dragonoid is the first evolved version of this powerful dragonlike beast. After its transformation, Delta Dragonoid has a cobralike hood around its head and sharp thorns all over its body. It also gets a lot more Gs, making it harder to beat on the field.

Dan's Drago evolves into a Delta Dragonoid in the episode "Drago's on Fire!"

EL CONDOR

This strange-looking warrior may resemble a wooden totem pole, but it's not. El Condor is a Bakugan that has the ability to fly. Prepare for an attack from above if you're battling against El Condor. This Bakugan will take flight, soaring high above you to launch its assault.

In "Duel in the Desert," Komba used his Ventus El Condor to beat Shun's Falconeer.

EXEDRA

Who said two heads are better than one? It couldn't have been Exedra because this Bakugan knows that eight heads is the way to go. One of the six soldiers of Vestroia, this legendary Darkus Bakugan resembles a multiheaded snake.

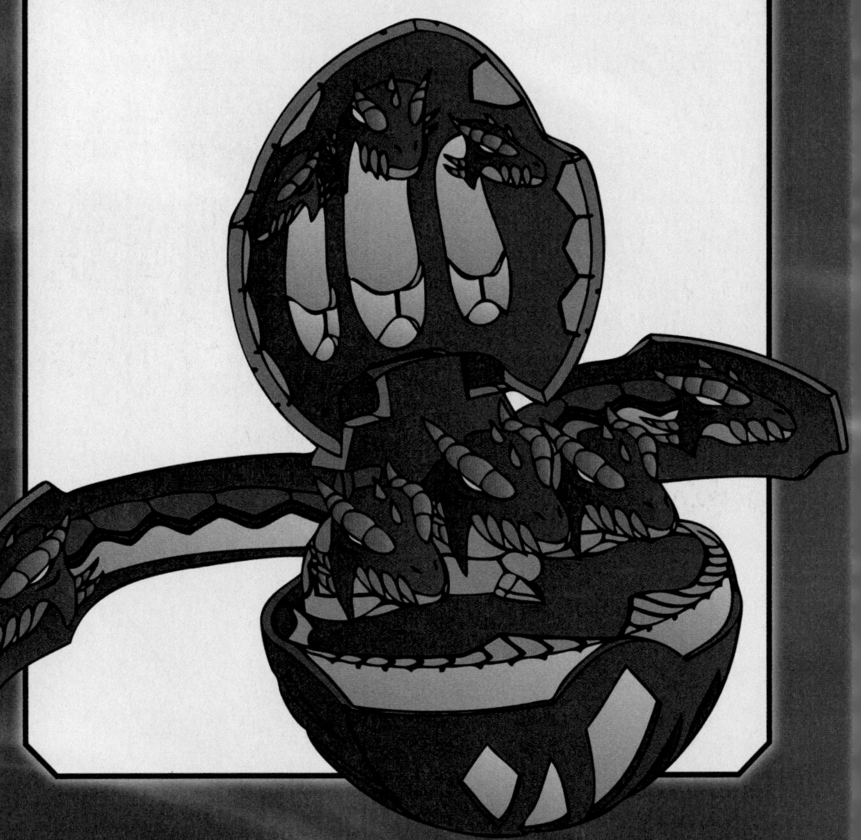

FALCONEER

Terror from above! This Bakugan targets its prey from the sky. Magical and mysterious, Falconeer has powerful psychic abilities that enables it to see through things, no matter how far away or what may be blocking it. If you defeat Falconeer, don't celebrate just yet. This phoenix-like creature can resurrect itself and heal any damage it may have obtained.

Shuji may be a big bully, but he has some awesome Bakugan. His Ventus Falconeer is hard to beat.

FEAR RIPPER

Fear Ripper is built to attack—its hands are sharp, giant blades. And Fear Ripper knows exactly how to use them. On the field, he attacks swiftly and ferociously.

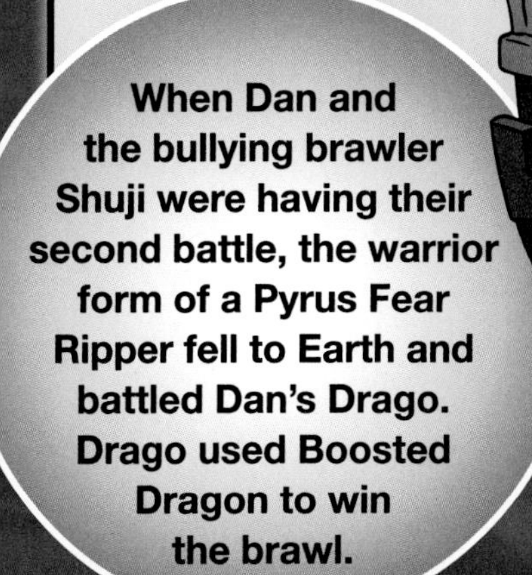

When Dan and the bullying brawler Shuji were having their second battle, the warrior form of a Pyrus Fear Ripper fell to Earth and battled Dan's Drago. Drago used Boosted Dragon to win the brawl.

FOURTRESS

How do you defend yourself against a Fourtress attack? It all depends on which one of its three faces you are looking at. Each face gives Fourtress different abilities: sorrow, gentleness, or anger. If this Bakugan is fighting for you, it's sure to lend a hand. It's got four arms!

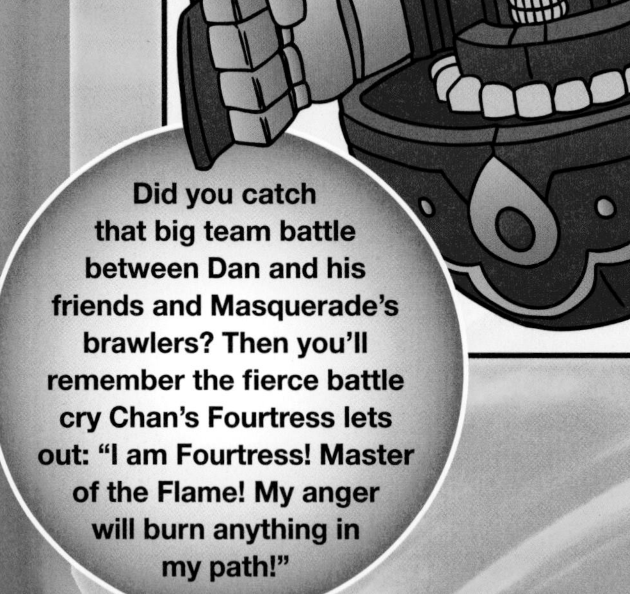

Did you catch that big team battle between Dan and his friends and Masquerade's brawlers? Then you'll remember the fierce battle cry Chan's Fourtress lets out: "I am Fourtress! Master of the Flame! My anger will burn anything in my path!"

FROSCH

You'll certainly be hoppy if you have this Bakugan on your team! The froglike Frosch is a legendary Aquos Bakugan and one of the six soldiers of Vestroia. Frosch is extremely wise and known for its strategic battle plan.

GARGONOID

If Gargonoid isn't moving, you might mistake it for a gargoyle. Its face and powerful wings make it look like one of these stone creatures. But you won't find Gargonoid sitting on top of a roof. Like all Bakugan, this warrior loves to brawl!

GOREM

This gigantic Bakugan resembles a walking piece of rock! Attacks bounce right off the tough and hard Gorem. The Ability Card Mega Impact gives Gorem an extra power boost of 50 Gs.

Julie was so lonely! All of her friends had talking Bakugan, and she didn't have any. Then Gorem heard her cry, and reached out a rocky hand to be Julie's friend. Julie thinks Gorem is the best Bakugan a girl ever had!

GRIFFON

The Griffon looks like it was made from three different creatures. It has the body of a lion, wings of an eagle, and the tail of a reptile.

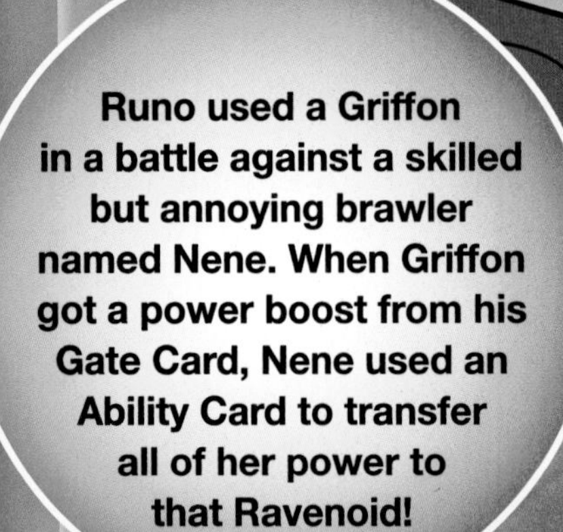

HAMMER GOREM

The evolved form of Gorem, Hammer Gorem, packs quite a punch. This Bakugan is stronger and more powerful when it evolves. In fact, its rocklike body becomes even harder, making Gorem tough to take down.

HARPUS

Harpus is quite a sight when she unfurls her large, feathered wings.

Komba's Ventus Harpus spits out insults that are even sharper than her claws! She rudely trash-talks her opponents on the field.

HYDRANOID

Hydranoid is a hulking dragonlike beast with sharp spikes all over its body. It is even more ferocious than it looks. This vicious Bakugan is known for being cruel and merciless in battle. It takes pleasure in pounding opponents with its tail.

Every time Masquerade sends a Bakugan to the Doom Dimension, his Darkus Hydranoid gets stronger.

HYNOID

The four-legged Hynoid looks like a hyena with a bad attitude.

Billy's Hynoid battles Julie's Rattleoid in the episode "A Perfect Match."

JUGGERNOID

A Juggernoid is like a walking Bakugan fortress. The heavily armored beast is almost impossible to injure. Many a brawler has tried and failed to take down the Juggernoid. It's hard to find even the smallest weakness in its armor.

This Bakugan isn't all about defense. A blow from Juggernoid will leave its opponents reeling, while sending shockwaves throughout the Bakugan universe.

A Juggernoid makes an appearance in the episode "The Secret of Success." He bonds with a young brawler named Christopher who has lost his confidence to battle.

LASERMAN

Built-in lasers provide the perfect weapon for Laserman. This robotic Bakugan comes armed and ready to brawl.

LIMULUS

Ouch! The sharp spikes on Limulus's back are very sharp—better not touch. That's not all this Bakugan has going for it. Limulus's entire body is covered in heavy-duty armor that's tough to crack.

Marucho used a Limulus in his battle against ace brawler Klaus.

MANION

The mysterious Manion resembles a sphinx with an elegant face and lean lion's body.

Chan uses the Ability Card Amun-Re to increase her Manion's G-power by a whopping 100 points.

MANTRIS

The stealthy Mantris can easily sneak up on its prey and pounce. Once this Bakugan has got its sharp claws into you, you won't stand a chance!

When Dan first battled Shuji, Shuji used a Subterra Mantris to take down Dan's Pyrus Serpenoid.

MONARUS

Don't let the pretty Monarus fool you. Just because this Bakugan resembles a butterfly with its beautiful wings doesn't mean it can't do real damage in a brawl.

In a battle against Masquerade, Hydranoid was about to send Drago to the Doom Dimension. Shun sacrificed his Monarus to save Drago.

OBERUS

Kindness can have its place on the battlefield. Just ask Oberus. This Bakugan is known for its compassion. The mothlike Oberus is a legendary Ventus Bakugan and one of the six soldiers of Vestroia.

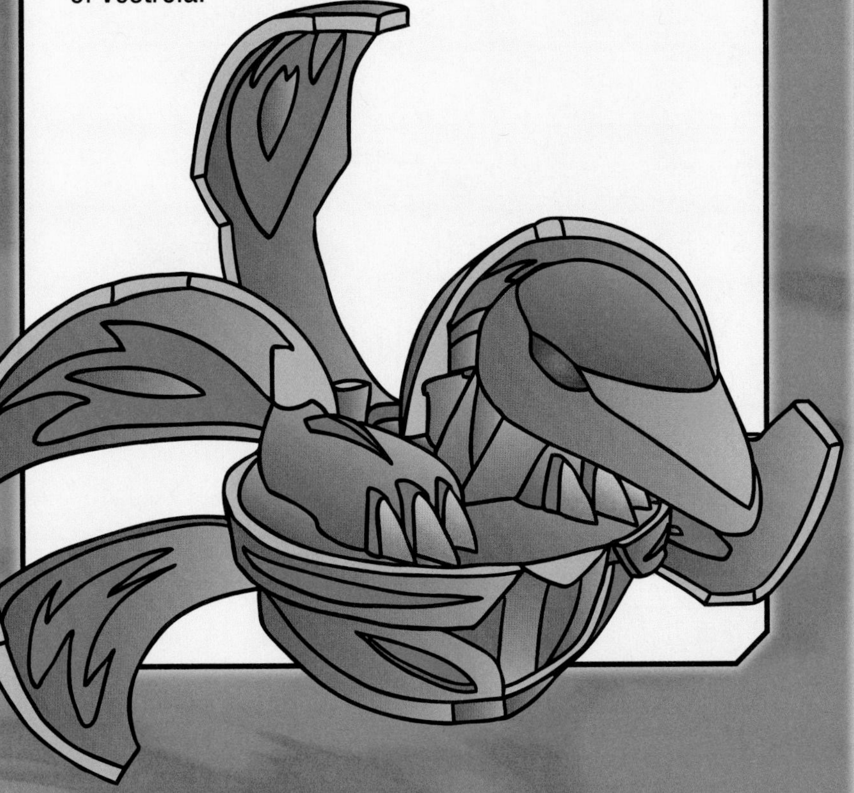

PREYAS

Preyas has the amazing ability to change attributes whenever it needs to. You'll find that this versatile Bakugan can be a huge help in battle.

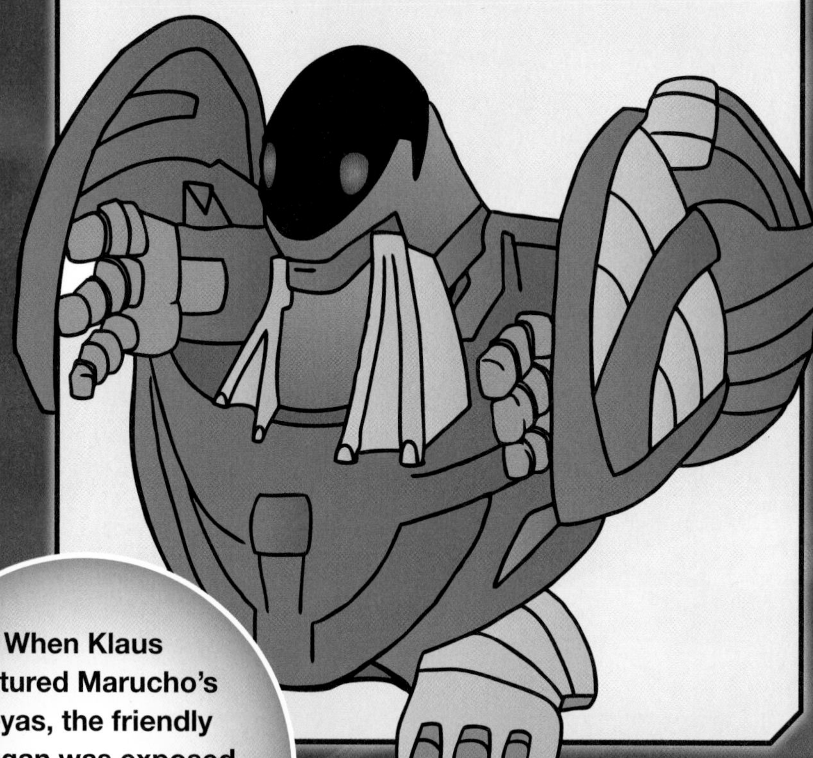

When Klaus captured Marucho's Preyas, the friendly Bakugan was exposed to negative energy. It briefly turned Preyas from a good guy into a real jerk!

RATTLEOID

Rattleoid and Serpenoid look a lot alike. They're both huge, fierce, snakelike creatures. How to tell the difference? Rattleoid has armor on its head, and a rattle on the end of its tail.

Brawler Billy likes to use an Ability Card called Poison Fang with his Rattleoid. It increases Rattleoid's Gs by 50 points—and the opposing Bakugan loses 50 points.

RAVENOID

A Ravenoid might look like a bird, but it's got some heavy-duty extra protection. Its entire body is covered in plated armor.

In the episode "My Good Friend," Julio's Tentaclear sent Runo's Ravenoid into the Doom Dimension.

REAPER

Here's some advice every brawler should heed: Never, ever make a Reaper angry at you. A Reaper will slowly wait, letting its rage build and build until the time is right. Then the Bakugan will explode, getting even with its foes by delivering devastating blow after blow. The cruel Reaper takes great pride in getting its revenge by unleashing a powerful fury.

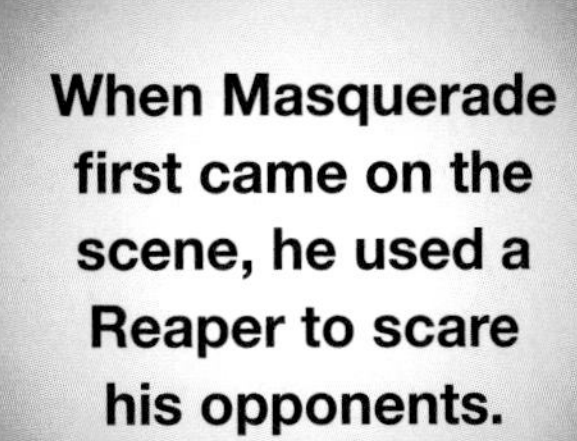

When Masquerade first came on the scene, he used a Reaper to scare his opponents.

ROBOTALLIAN

You are a lucky brawler if a Robotallian has got your back. The most important thing to this Bakugan is serving and protecting its friends. And Robotallian is one powerful bodyguard to have. With its fierce claws and gigantic blades that are capable of slicing through almost any material, this Bakugan will let nothing get in the way of its sense of duty.

The loyal Robotallian has another special talent. It can move at lightning-fast speeds that are hard to see with the human eye.

Dan had a Robotallian. He lost it to the Doom Dimension battling against Julio.

SAURUS

No frills. No fuss. Saurus doesn't worry about strategy or fancy camouflage. This Bakugan comes out swinging, using brute force alone to subdue its opponents. What does a Saurus make of challengers who believe they stand a chance? Nothing makes this tough Bakugan happier than to smash a hopeful foe into nothing.

After losing to Masquerade, Runo battled one of Masquerade's brawlers, Tetsuya. She teamed up her Haos Saurus with her Haos Tigrerra to win the match.

SERPENOID

The slow squeeze is Serpenoid's method of choice to subdue its enemies. This snakelike Bakugan wraps itself around a foe and slowly and painfully squeezes. Serpenoid will drain energy as it does this, making itself stronger while sucking all of its enemy's power. You'll often see Serpenoid slithering on the ground, but watch out. It can spring up and attack without a moment's notice.

Dan used his Pyrus Serpenoid in his first battle against Shuji, a local bully. Serpenoid put the squeeze on Shuji's Mantris, but didn't have enough Gs to win the brawl.

SIEGE

If you are ever in trouble during a brawl, Siege can be the Bakugan in shining armor that saves you! Siege is fully protected thanks to its suit of armor. It lashes at opponents with its long, sharp lance.

SIRENOID

The graceful Sirenoid is quite a catch for any brawler! The mermaidlike Bakugan wears long, flowing robes and protects herself with the harp she carries.

When Marucho's Preyas first saw Sirenoid, he thought she was beautiful. He soon realized how deadly that beauty could be. With the help of the Ability Card Anthemusa, Sirenoid sang a song that pulled Preyas right into the Doom Dimension.

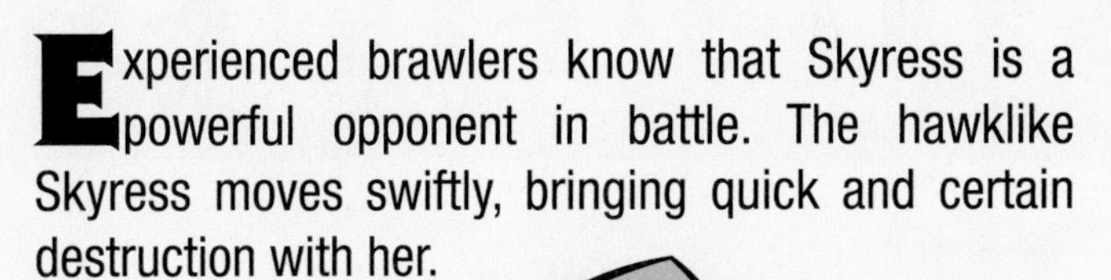

SKYRESS

Experienced brawlers know that Skyress is a powerful opponent in battle. The hawklike Skyress moves swiftly, bringing quick and certain destruction with her.

Shun's Skyress is smart and kind, and often gives Shun good advice.

STINGSLASH

When this Bakugan lashes out with its tail, opponents feel the sting. Stingslash looks like a scorpion with a humanoid face—pretty creepy! But looks don't matter when your warrior is delivering damage on the field.

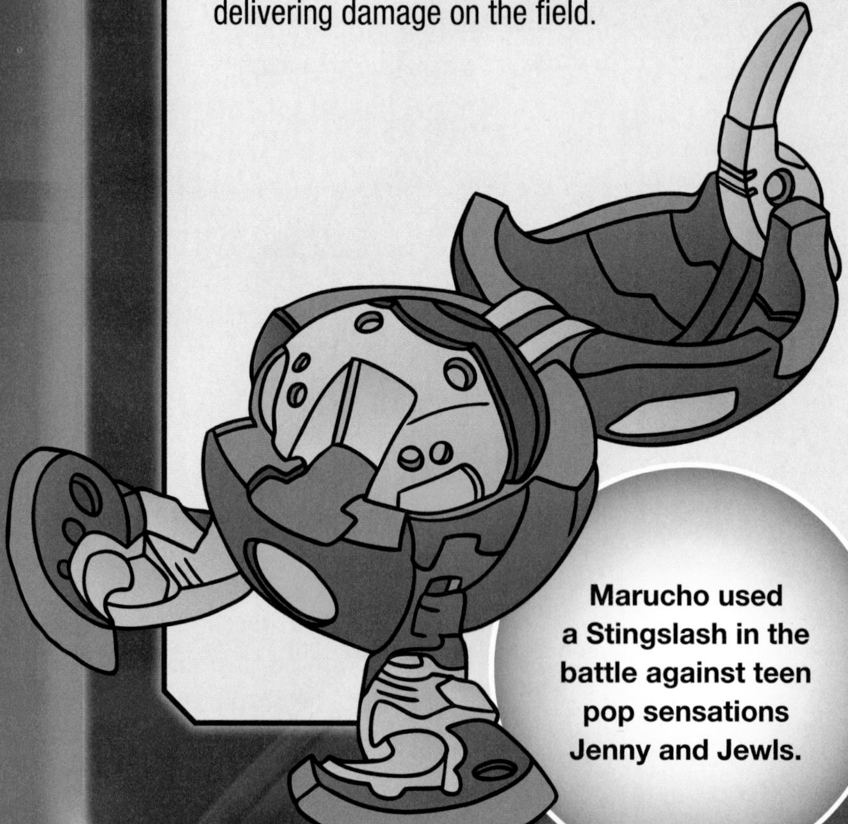

Marucho used a Stingslash in the battle against teen pop sensations Jenny and Jewls.

STORM SKYRESS

When Skyress evolves into Storm Skyress, she becomes bigger, stronger, and even more powerful.

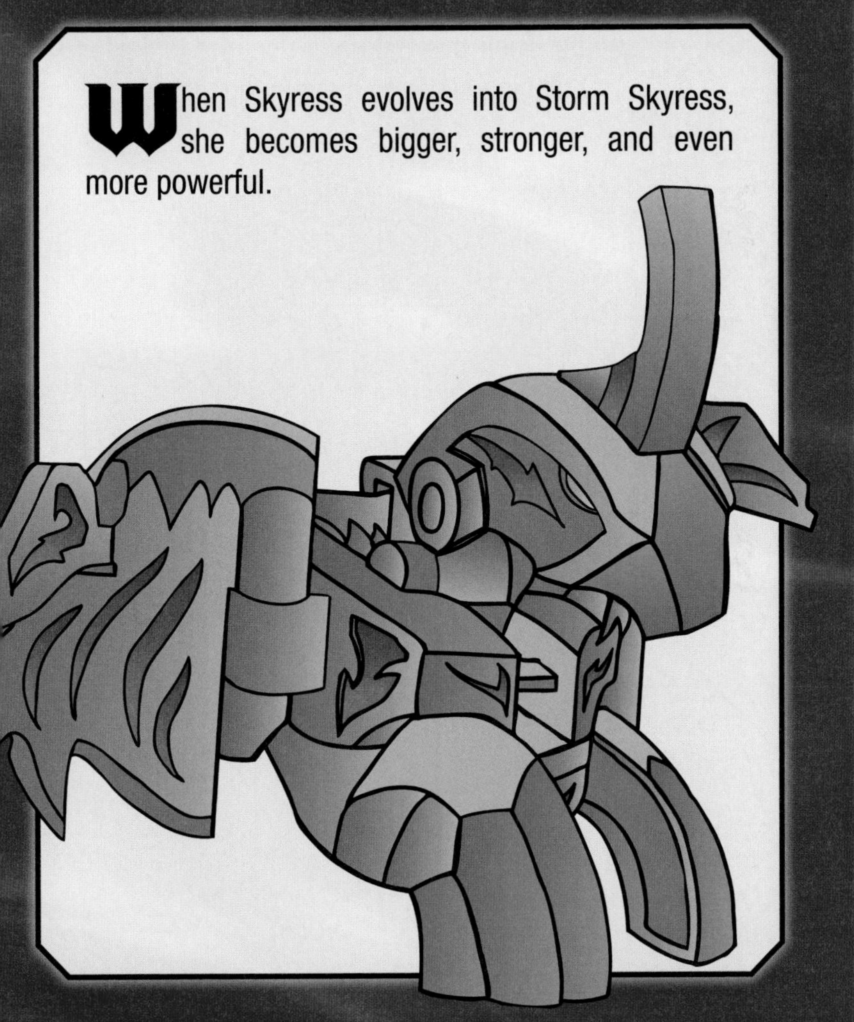

TENTACLEAR

One eye is all Tentaclear needs. It shoots a blazing laser beam from its single eye, blinding its opponents. Then this Bakugan uses its tentacles to deliver punishing blows to its stunned enemy.

TERRORCLAW

Feeling crabby? Maybe you've encountered this crablike Bakugan in a brawl. Terrorclaw's large, sharp claws can shred its enemies.

TIGRERRA

Here, kitty kitty! An agile and fast Bakugan, Tigrerra pounces on its prey with ease. This tigerlike terror is armored for protection.

Runo's Haos Tigrerra and Dan's Drago are good friends.

TUSKOR

Tuskor will come barreling at any challenger, baring its two large and lethal tusks. An Ability Card called Nose Slap allows Tuskor to battle a Bakugan standing on another Gate Card.

WARIUS

This extreme warrior takes no prisoners. Tall and strong, Warius carries a heavy-duty mace that it uses to smash its foes.

WAVERN

Shining white Wavern is a wise and kind Bakugan. She is Naga's twin, and they couldn't be more opposite. She holds the positive energy of the Infinity Core inside of her, while Naga has swallowed up the negative Silent Core.

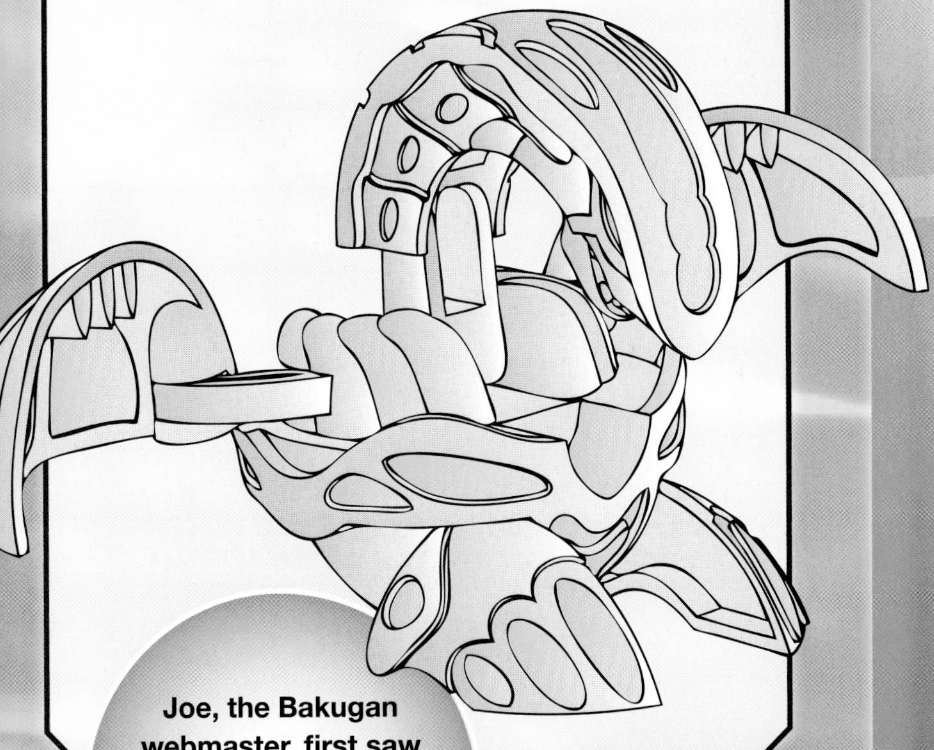

Joe, the Bakugan webmaster, first saw Wavern in a dream. She warned him that Naga must never get the Infinity Core.

WORMQUAKE

This is one worm you don't want to use as bait—unless you're trying to capture a really big and scary Bakugan! Wormquake is a gigantic worm that has a huge, scary mouth filled with painfully sharp teeth.

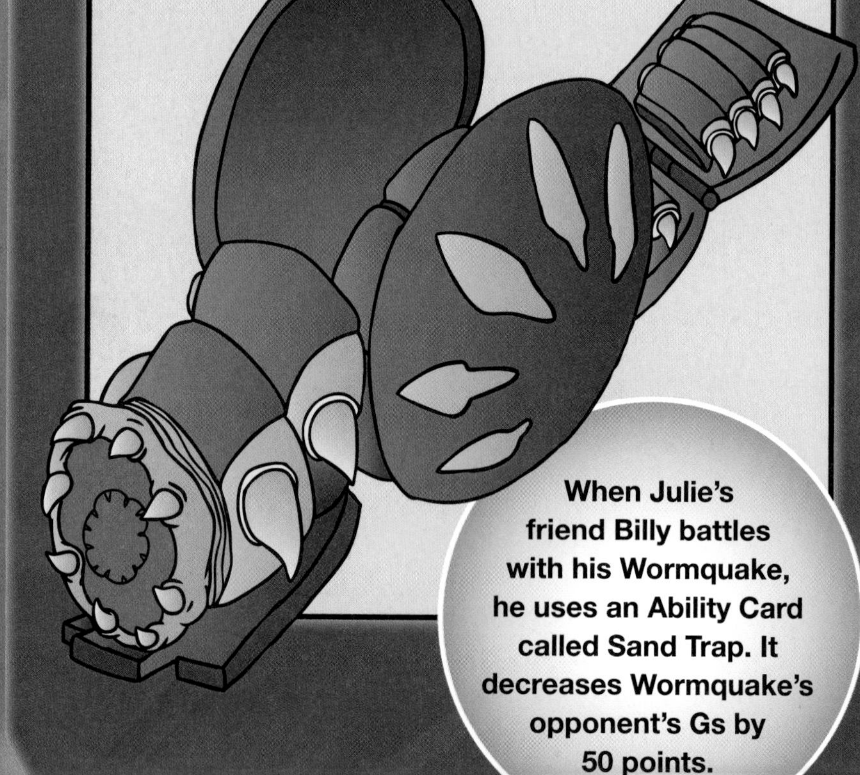

When Julie's friend Billy battles with his Wormquake, he uses an Ability Card called Sand Trap. It decreases Wormquake's opponent's Gs by 50 points.

>>> BRAWLING BASICS

Want to be a Bakugan brawler? You'll need skill, strategy and guts—but those things will come the more you practice. To get started, all you need are some Bakugan Gate Cards and Bakugan balls. In this section you'll learn how to brawl with your Bakugan two ways: super fast Speed Play and multiplayer Arena Play. First though, you need to learn how to use your cards and balls.

>>> BAKUGAN BALLS

When Bakugan come to the human world, they lose their warrior form. They transform into Bakugan balls. Inside each ball is a warrior waiting to get out.

To free your Bakugan warrior, you must shoot the ball onto the playing field. When the ball stops, it should open up, revealing your warrior. When this happens, your Bakugan "stands."

When your Bakugan stands, you can see a number inside the ball. This number is your Bakugan's G Power. It's an important number. When you play Bakugan, the warrior with the most G Power wins the brawl. Don't worry if your Bakugan ball has low G Power. You can use your Bakugan cards to give your beast a boost!

>>>> BAKUGAN

GATE CARDS

You can't play Bakugan without Bakugan Gate Cards. These cards form the Bakugan playing field. There are four types of Bakugan cards.

Each Bakugan card has two sides. The Sector side is the "back" of the card. The Holo Sector side has a symbol for each of the six planets on it. Inside each symbol is a + or – number. This number shows the G Power that will be added or subtracted from the Bakugan standing on it.

There is one more number on the Holo Sector side: the HSP. This number shows the number of Holo Sector Points the card has. At the end of a battle, these points will be added up to help determine the overall winner.

NORMAL:

This card has six G-Power boosts and HSP.

COMMAND:

This card has extra instructions players must follow in addition to adding or subtracting the G-Power boosts.

CHARACTER:

A Bakugan's G Power doubles when it stands on its own character card.

ABILITY:

This card has a special command that players must follow in addition to adding or subtracting the G-Power boosts.

Speed Play

To play Speed Play, you need two players and at least one Bakugan and one Gate Card each. You can brawl once or keep brawling until both players' cards are gone. At the end of the game, the player with the most HSPs (Holo Sector Points) is the winner.

STEP 1: BEGIN

The youngest player goes first—that's Player 1. Player 1 throws down a card, facedown.

STEP 2: SHOOT

Player 1 shoots a Bakugan. If Player 1's ball lands on the card, Player 1 is good to go. If Player 1's ball does not land on the card, Player 1 has to wait to shoot again until the next turn. Either way, Player 2 is up.

How to Shoot Your Bakugan

Make sure your Bakugan is two card lengths away from the facedown card. Then toss your Bakugan onto the field.

STEP 3: BRAWL!

Player 2 shoots a Bakugan. Player 1 and Player 2 take turns until they each have a Bakugan standing on the card. Then it's time to brawl! Look at the number showing on each Bakugan. That number tells you how many Gs each Bakugan has.

WHAT HAPPENS IF...

...one player has two Bakugan stand on the same card? That player automatically captures the card.

STEP 4: TURN OVER THE GATE CARD

Now it's time to turn over the Gate Card. Look at the six G-Power boosts on the card. Match the G-Power boost to the planet your Bakugan comes from. Add or subtract those points from your Bakugan's Gs. For example, if you have a Pyrus Bakugan with 200 Gs, and the power boost on the Pyrus symbol is +50, now your Bakugan has 250 Gs.

STEP 5: ADD IT UP

Now Player 1 and Player 2 compare to see whose Bakugan has the most Gs. The player whose Bakugan has a higher number of Gs gets to keep the card—and the Bakugan.

WHAT HAPPENS IF . . .

. . . there is a tie? Then each player keeps their Bakugan and the card is taken out of play.

STEP 6: MORE ROUNDS

End of round one! If you want to keep playing, Player 2 throws down a card and the brawling starts all over again. The player who won the last brawl shoots first. A couple of catches: You can't brawl with any Bakugan you've captured, only the Bakugan you brought to the battle. Also, once a card has been thrown, it can't be thrown again.

STEP 7: TAKE TURNS

Both players take turns throwing down cards until all cards are captured. When you're done brawling, it's time to figure out who the winner is.

STEP 8: COUNT YOUR HSPS

Each player needs to count up their HSP points. First, total up the HSPs on each of the cards you have captured. Then, add 100 HSPs for each Bakugan you have. The player with the most HSPs wins!

BE A GOOD SPORT: Bakugan warriors and cards are captured during game play only! After the game is over, players should return the Bakugan and Gate Cards they have captured to their opponent.

PLAYER 1:	PLAYER 2:
Gate Cards: 850 HSPs	Gate Cards: 600 HSPs
Captured Bakugan: 300 HSPs	Captured Bakugan: 400 HSPs
TOTAL: 1150 HSPS	**TOTAL: 1000 HSPS**

PLAYER 1 WINS!

Arena Play

For Arena Play, you need 2–4 players. Each player must use the same number of Bakugan and Gate Cards in the battle. There is a minimum of three Gate Cards for each player. No matter how many cards are used, only one of them can be an Ability Card.

STEP 1: BAKUGAN FIELD!

Each player lays one card facedown on the field, on the opposite side of the playing area from where the player is. The first card played may not be an Ability Card.

WHAT HAPPENS IF . . .

. . . there are only two players? Then each player lays down two cards to start.

STEP 2: SHOOT!

The youngest player shoots first. Two things can happen: The Bakugan can stand on the card, or it will miss. If you miss, you keep your Bakugan. If you stand, your card stays on the field until its time to brawl. Either way, you can lay down a new card on the field if you have one.

After the first player goes, play continues counterclockwise around the field.

WHAT HAPPENS IF . . .

. . . your Bakugan knocks a standing Bakugan off of a card—and then stands on that card? You win the brawl!

STEP 3: BRAWL!

If two Bakugan stand on the same card, it's time to brawl! Turn over the Gate Card underneath the Bakugan. Brawling happens the same way it does in Speed Play: Turn over the Gate Card and add up the Gs. The player whose Bakugan has the most G points wins the brawl. That player captures the card and the opponent's Bakugan.

WHAT HAPPENS IF . . .

. . . the G points for both Bakugan are the same? Time for Sudden Fury! Each player takes back their Bakugan. The Gate Card is left Holo Sector side up. Then both players shoot at the same time. If both players miss, the card stays on the field for the next round. If only one player stands, that player wins the brawl. If both players stand, it's Sudden Fury all over again!

STEP 4: CALLING STAY

When you have no more Bakugans to shoot, you may call stay. Choose a Bakugan that is standing on a card and call "Stay." If no other Bakugan stands on that card during the round, you capture the card—and win back your Bakugan.

STEP 5: CROWNING A WINNER

Players take turns shooting Bakugan until all the Bakugan and Gate Cards have been captured—or when only one player has Bakugan left to shoot. As in Speed Play, everyone adds up the HSP points on their captured cards. Then add 100 points for each Bakugan you have. The player with the highest HSP wins the game!

BRAWLING TIPS

You have control over what Bakugan you use and what cards you throw out. Say you're using an Aquos Bakugan. Start with a Gate Card that gives Aquos Bakugan a big boost. Then try to aim for that Gate Card. When you brawl, you'll have the advantage.

Landing on the card you want isn't as easy as it looks. It takes skill. Practice shooting in your spare time. Then when it's time to brawl, you'll be more accurate.

Think about specializing in Bakugan aligned with one planet, like Pyrus or Subterra. If you have all Subterra warriors and all of your Gate Cards give extra power to Subterra Bakugan, you'll have a better chance of landing on a Gate Card that will help you.

Brawl as often as you can! The more you brawl, the better you'll get to know your Bakugan.

TEN BEST
>>>> BRAWLS

"BAKUGAN FIELD OPEN!"

Those three words send a chill of excitement through every Bakugan brawler. Time comes to a stop all around you as the Bakugan field is formed with Gate Cards. Once the field is set, it's time to brawl!

What makes a brawl exciting? Sometimes, it's the Bakugan warriors in the battle. It's a real thrill to see a powerful beast that you've never seen before. Sometimes, it's the strategy the players use. There's nothing like it when a brawler is just about to lose—and then whips out an Ability Card to win it all. Other times, it's all about the brawlers. Even a bad brawler can help to make an entertaining battle.

In this section you'll read about the ten best Bakugan brawls—so far. As long as brawlers keep challenging each other, this list will keep getting longer!

DAN VS. SHUJI:

Dan's first battle with big bully Shuji was pretty typical. Shuji used a bunch of big Bakugan he didn't know how to battle with, and Dan wiped the field with him pretty quickly.

But Dan's second battle with Shuji is one to remember. Why? It's the first time Dan and Drago ever battled together.

Dan and Shuji were locked in a rematch. Dan's Pyrus Serpenoid was wrapped around Shuji's Darkus Stingslash. Dan needed more power, so he used an Ability Card called Quartet Battle. With this card, both he and Shuji could bring another Bakugan into the battle.

At that very moment, the gate between Vestroia and Earth opened up. Fear Ripper and Drago fell through the gate and joined the battle. Drago battled for Dan. He tried to reason with Fear Ripper, but the Darkus Bakugan wouldn't listen. So Drago used Boosted Dragon to boost Fear Ripper right out of the match!

CHRISTOPHER VS. TRAVIS:

This battle makes the list because it's an inspiring story for brawlers everywhere.

Christopher was a young brawler just learning about Bakugan. A bully named Travis forced Christopher to brawl every day—and Christopher lost every single time. He was ready to give up Bakugan.

Then Alice ran into Christopher one day and heard his story. Alice realized Christopher just needed some confidence to beat Travis. She went to Christopher's next battle as his coach. A strange rip in time took Alice away from the field, but Christopher was able to hear Alice's voice.

"It's not always about skill and brawn," Alice told him. "Confidence wins battles!"

Christopher listened. He didn't lose confidence, even when he lost a round. In the end, he was down to only one Bakugan: his Juggernoid. But with help from Alice, and faith in himself, he beat Travis—and earned his respect.

RUNO VS. TATSUYA:

Runo was one of Masquerade's first victims. It made her really angry when the masked brawler sent her Bakugan to the Doom Dimension. She wanted revenge.

Then one day she accidentally picked up Dan's Baku-Pod and saw a message from Masquerade asking to battle. Seeing her chance, she ran to the battle site. She didn't find Masquerade—he sent another brawler in his place, a boy named Tatsuya.

Runo didn't care. She would get her revenge no matter what. Runo lost her Juggernoid early in the battle, and her Haos Tigrerra begged to be put on the field. But Runo had a strategy, and she was patient. She took out Tatsuya's Garganoid and Griffon. She still had her Haos Saurus and Haos Tigrerra left. That's when Tatsuya tossed out his secret weapon—a fierce Fear Ripper.

Runo had a plan. She sent out Tigrerra to help Saurus. With a little boost from a Crystal Fang ability card, Tigrerra defeated Fear Ripper. Runo won the match—but she still had a score to settle with Masquerade.

JULIE VS. BILLY:

Julie and Billy have been friends since they were young kids. Then Bakugan came along, and they both became brawlers. Julie couldn't wait to challenge her old friend in battle.

The first time they brawled, Billy won, thanks to his Cycloid. Julie felt jealous that Billy had a talking Bakugan and she didn't. She went searching in the Bakugan Valley and didn't find anything but spiders and dust.

Back in her room, she opened up her heart to her feelings about wanting a Bakugan. That's when her Bakugan Subterra Gorem started to talk to her. Julie was thrilled. She had found her Baku-partner at last!

She asked Billy for a rematch. Cycloid and Gorem went head-to-head—two powerhouses on the field. First, Julie used Mega Impact to increase Gorem's power by 50 Gs. Then Billy's Level Down Gate Card took away 100 points from Gorem. Cycloid attacked with his huge hammer—but Billy didn't know that Gorem was protected by a shield. Cycloid's Gs dropped every time he pounded Gorem. Julie's giant ended the battle with one powerful punch.

CHAN LEE VS. DAN:

Chan Lee was the third-ranked Bakugan player in the world—and under Masquerade's control. When she challenged Dan to a battle, Dan's friends didn't want him to take her on alone. They thought she was too tough to beat. But Dan wanted to battle Chan Lee—even though she held the Doom Card. If Dan lost, he would never see Drago again.

Dan started out strong. His Mantris knocked out Chan Lee's first two Bakugan. Then Chan Lee released her fierce Fourtress and sent Mantris to the Doom Dimension.

Chan Lee had another surprise for Dan. She used a card called Revive to bring her defeated Bakugan back on the field. Chan Lee had three Bakugan left, and Dan had Siege and Drago.

Fourtress quickly took care of Siege. Drago got rid of the other two Bakugan. Then it was Fourtress and Drago in a head-to-head match. It looked like Drago might be sent to the Doom Dimension when he started to burn hot with a mysterious new power. Drago blasted Fourtress off the field, and Dan won the match against Chan Lee. She vowed to defeat him the next time they battled.

MASQUERADE VS. HIS MINIONS:

Masquerade loved to have other brawlers do his dirty work for him. One way or another he convinced Billy, Klaus, Julio, Chan Lee, and Komba to join his quest to send Bakugan to the Doom Dimension.

When Masquerade was finished with his minions, he turned on them. He battled each of them one by one—and defeated them all, using only his Hydranoid! He cackled with glee as their Bakugan were sent to the Doom Dimension.

He took care of Julio first. Then he moved on to Chan Lee. She used her Centipoid, Warius, and Fourtress, but Hydranoid beat them all.

Komba was Masquerade's next target. His Harpus battled fiercely for him, but Masquerade used a move called Fusion Ability to void Harpus' Feather Blast.

Billy lost his good friend Cycloid in the next brawl. Masquerade finished with the arrogant Klaus. He didn't want to use his Sirenoid in battle, but she disobeyed his orders. She put herself in the brawl and sacrificed herself for Klaus. His heart was broken. But Masquerade's work was done.

MASQUERADE AND SHUN  DAN:

Shun was the number-one ranked Bakugan player for awhile, but he gave it up. Dan's friends tried to get Shun back in the game to help them defeat Masquerade. But when Dan went looking for Shun, Masquerade was there—tempting Shun with the power of the Doom Card.

A three-way brawl began, with Masquerade and Shun working together to take Dan down. Or at least, that's what it looked like. Masquerade brought out his Hydranoid for the first time during this battle. He was about to send Drago to the Doom Dimension when Shun sacrificed his Monarus to save Drago!

The tables slowly turned on Masquerade. Dan and Shun teamed up to take down Hydranoid. Skyress distracted him while Drago aimed a fire attacked right in Hydranoid's mouth. Masquerade lost the brawl, and Skyress and Drago now faced each other. Drago was victorious—and Shun was back in the game. He agreed to help Dan and his friends defeat Masquerade once and for all.

DAN & MARUCHO VS. JENNY & JEWLS:

This fun brawl was filled with twists and turns. It started at a party at Marucho's new (gigantic) house. First, Preyas decided he wanted to live large with Marucho, so he became Marucho's Bakugan. Then Jenny and Jewls rang the doorbell. The teen pop singing sensations longed to play Bakugan, but their manager wouldn't let them. Then Masquerade tempted them with the Doom Card and sent them to battle Dan.

Marucho joined Dan against the girls in a combination battle. Watching the brawl was like getting a lesson in Bakugan strategy. Jenny battled with Aquos Bakugan, and Jewls battled with Subterra Bakugan. They used diagonal moves to combine the elements of their warriors to give them extra power.

Dan and Marucho followed their lead and teamed up, too. At first, they weren't sure if Preyas would be a team player. He was busy showing off and doing his own thing. But in the end, Preyas and Drago joined forces to defeat Jenny and Jewls' Bakugan.

DAN, MARUCHO, AND RUNO VS. KLAUS, CHAN, AND JULIO:

Crazy for power, Naga wanted to get rid of Drago so he could find the Infinity Core. Marucho's minions, Klaus, Chan, and Julio, vowed to defeat Drago for their master, Masquerade. The three of them challenged Dan, Marucho, and Runo to a triple battle.

The battle started off with a shock. Klaus was brawling with Marucho's Preyas! Preyas hadn't gone to the Doom Dimension after all—he had been captured by Klaus. Dosed with negative energy, Preyas had become a monster.

Marucho wanted Preyas back so badly he didn't think. He sent out Bakugan after Bakugan and lost them all. He and Dan and Runo began to argue. Finally, Runo's Tigrerra straightened them out. She told them to work as a team, or they'd never win.

The brawlers listened. They worked together to take down their opponents' Bakugan. In the end, Runo used a card called Pure Light to get Preyas back from Klaus. Preyas was back to normal, and Marucho was happy to have his good friend back.

DAN VS. MASQUERADE:

Joe informed Dan and his friends that Masquerade was coming for them—and that Masquerade's powerful Hydranoid had evolved.

Masquerade showed up, as promised, and the brawl began. First up was Masquerade's Darkus Wormquake against Dan's Pyrus Griffon. Griffon won that battle.

Masquerade sent out Darkus Laserman next. Dan used Griffon again—and Griffon lost even before the brawl began. Masquerade used a Joker's Wild Gate Card, which allowed Darkus Bakugan to automatically win the brawl.

Laserman took care of Dan's Saurus next with Quicksand Freeze. That's when Dan's Drago took the field to face off against Masquerade's Dual Hydranoid. The fight raged on, with each Bakugan delivering damage to the other. Dan used a Gate Card that doubled Drago's power. But before he could attack, Masquerade used Destruction Impact and obliterated all of those Gs. That left Drago helpless.

Dual Hydranoid sent Drago to the Doom Dimension. Dan couldn't bear to see Drago go alone, so he ran after his friend. They disappeared together.

YOUR BAKUGAN

Here's a great way to improve your game! Keep track of the Bakugan you get and the cards you use with them. Before you brawl, check over your stats to plan your strategy.

BAKUGAN NAME: ______________________

PLANETARY ATTRIBUTE: ______________________

WARRIOR CLASS: ______________________

GATE CARDS TO USE WITH THIS BAKUGAN:

____

____

____

____

ABILITY CARDS TO USE WITH THIS BAKUGAN:

____

____

____

____

WINS: ______________________

LOSSES: ______________________

BAKUGAN NAME: ______________________

PLANETARY ATTRIBUTE: ________________

WARRIOR CLASS: _____________________

GATE CARDS TO USE WITH THIS BAKUGAN:

____

____

____

____

____

____

ABILITY CARDS TO USE WITH THIS BAKUGAN:

____

____

____

____

____

____

WINS: ______________________________

LOSSES: ____________________________

BAKUGAN NAME: ______________________________

PLANETARY ATTRIBUTE: ______________________

WARRIOR CLASS: ____________________________

GATE CARDS TO USE WITH THIS BAKUGAN:

____

____

____

____

____

____

ABILITY CARDS TO USE WITH THIS BAKUGAN:

____

____

____

____

____

____

WINS: ______________________________________

LOSSES: ____________________________________

BAKUGAN NAME: ______________________

PLANETARY ATTRIBUTE: ______________________

WARRIOR CLASS: ______________________

GATE CARDS TO USE WITH THIS BAKUGAN:

____

____

____

____

____

____

ABILITY CARDS TO USE WITH THIS BAKUGAN:

____

____

____

____

____

____

WINS: ______________________

LOSSES: ______________________

BAKUGAN NAME: ______________________________

PLANETARY ATTRIBUTE: ______________________

WARRIOR CLASS: _____________________________

GATE CARDS TO USE WITH THIS BAKUGAN:

____

____

____

____

____

____

ABILITY CARDS TO USE WITH THIS BAKUGAN:

____

____

____

____

____

____

WINS: ____

LOSSES: _______________________________________